Donated by
Anna Steinbacher
1971

# Josefina February

# JOSEFINA FEBRUARY

written and illustrated by **EVALINE NESS**

CHARLES SCRIBNER'S SONS New York

$N$ot long ago on a high hill in Haiti there lived a little girl named Josefina February. Josefina lived with her grandfather, Mr. February, in a house that had one room, bamboo walls and a banana leaf roof.

In front of their house stood an enormous Silk-cotton tree
in which Josefina had her private sitting room. From her room

in the tree she could watch the sea a mile away, and the market place which was halfway to the sea.

In back of their house was the grove, surrounded by a cactus fence. In the grove there were oranges, breadfruit, bananas and yams; avocados, mangoes, pineapples and beans. Poppies, which grew everywhere, covered the ground and poinsettias ringed round the trunks of the calabash trees.

Early every morning Josefina and her grandfather went to
the grove and picked the fruit which had ripened overnight.
They carried the fruit in baskets on their heads and walked
down the hill to the market place. With the money they earned
from the fruit they sold, they bought candles and matches, salt

and soap, and sometimes calico. Mr. February always gave
Josefina a penny or two to spend as she pleased.

Josefina loved the market place. There was so much to see
and smell and hear. People, baskets, hats and mats were all
mixed in with coffee beans, sisal and rice. Bananas and yams,
meat and beans boiled in big black cauldrons over charcoal
fires. There were sugar-cane candies and coconuts. There were
beads, ribbons, combs and shoes; calabash bowls and wicker
chairs, and goats and oranges everywhere. Church bells rang,
donkeys brayed and children blew bamboo trumpets.

One morning, instead of going to market, Mr. February went to work all day in Mr. Hippolyte's sugar-cane fields. He told Josefina to play at home—but Josefina had other plans.

That day was her grandfather's birthday and Josefina wanted to buy him a pair of real leather shoes. She decided to go to the market alone. If she could sell one basket of fruit she would have enough money, with the pennies she had saved, to buy the shoes.

After her grandfather left, Josefina took her basket and went to the grove. While she was picking the oranges, mangoes, bananas and yams, she heard a strange sound. It seemed to come from the coffee berry bush. Josefina looked behind the bush and saw a little black burro, with a fringe of brown hair on top of his head that looked like a cap. His legs were so wobbly he could hardly stand and his ears looked as long as his legs.

Josefina picked him up and held him close. The little burro
folded his soft ears and put his head under Josefina's chin. She
decided to call him Cap.

She wondered if Cap belonged to someone. How she wished he belonged to her! She would teach him clever tricks. She would play games with him. And when he was older, she would ride on his back to the sea.

Josefina was so busy dreaming of the future, it was noon before she remembered the fruit she had picked to take to the market. She couldn't bear the thought of leaving Cap, so she decided to take him with her.

As she stood there in the noonday sun, Josefina suddenly felt cold. What if Cap belonged to the very first person she met? Would that be worse than the very last? First, last, last or first, it would be the same: if Cap belonged to someone else, he couldn't belong to her.

But perhaps he was like Josefina who had no mother, no father, no sister, no brother. Cap might not even have a grandfather. He might, just possibly, belong to no one in the whole world except Josefina!

Somehow she felt warmer, so she put her basket on her head, picked up Cap and started down the hill.

As she passed the cemetery, the first person she met was Lilly, the tallest, haughtiest girl on the hill. Lilly had a bandanna full of bananas on her head. "Pardon me, Lilly," Josefina said. "As you can see, I have a baby burro here. Does he belong to you?"

Lilly swept by without a word.

When Lilly had gone, Josefina whispered to Cap, "Well, any-way, it wasn't the *first* person."

She met no one else until she reached the bottom of the hill. There she saw a little girl and her brother who were selling oranges by the roadside. Josefina went up to them and said, "Pardon me. As you can see, I have a baby burro here. What do you think of him?"

The girl and her brother, as if they were one, said, "We wish he belonged to us!"

Josefina smiled and continued along the road. Suddenly she heard a croak, a cackle and a screech. She turned around and saw an old woman with three blackbirds. When Josefina asked, "Pardon me, have you lost a baby burro?" the old woman said not a word, but the three blackbirds cackled and croaked, "Not we not we not we!"

Josefina felt light with happiness. So far, no one belonged to Cap!

Soon she came to a house that looked like a kite on a string. Two sisters named Yvette and Yvonne were standing on the porch. Josefina walked up to them and asked politely, "Miss Yvette and Miss Yvonne, would you know anyone who might have lost a baby burro? This burro here?"

Yvette and Yvonne smiled at Josefina and simply said, "No, dear."

Josefina hugged Cap and hurried on to the market place. When she got there she could hardly believe her eyes. The market place was empty! All the people had taken their wares and gone home to supper.

Josefina didn't know what to do. She was happy and sad at the same time. Now Cap belonged to her, but she had not sold the fruit and she had no real leather shoes to give to her grandfather for his birthday.

She turned away from the market place and started to walk slowly home. As she passed Mr. Hippolyte's sugar-cane fields, she was surprised to hear her name called. It was Mr. Hippolyte himself leaning on the fence with his big straw hat resting on his nose.

Josefina tried to smile, but instead she started to cry. She cried so hard she thought she would never be able to stop long enough to tell Mr. Hippolyte her terrible trouble. Mr. Hippolyte just waited. At last Josefina wiped away her tears and told him her story.

Mr. Hippolyte looked at Josefina a long time. Then he said, "It just happens that I have a new pair of real leather shoes. Would you consider trading Cap for the shoes?"

It was Josefina's turn to look at Mr. Hippolyte a long time.
Then she nodded her head. She was afraid to speak for fear she
would cry again.

While she waited for Mr. Hippolyte to return with the shoes,
Josefina did cry a little more. She made two neat braids in Cap's
mane and tied them with the ribbons from her hair. She kissed
Cap's nose and told him to be good. She promised Cap she would
never, never forget him.

When Josefina got home it was almost dark. She cooked ham and yams in a big pot and cut up all the fruit from her basket for dessert. She had just put the shoes in the middle of the table when Mr. February walked in. He stood there and smiled at Josefina. And Josefina stood there and smiled back. Then Mr. February put on his real leather shoes and kissed Josefina on top of her head.

Mr. February and Josefina ate the birthday supper in silence. They had almost finished when Mr. February said, "Poor Mr. Hippolyte. He has a responsibility, not a very big one, but he thinks he cannot handle it alone. He wondered if you would like to take care of it for him."

Josefina stared at her grandfather. Mr. Hippolyte had a responsibility! She started to speak but before she could sa word, the door slowly opened.

And in wobbled a little black burro, fringed on top, with
ribbons in his mane.